JAN BRETT

HONEY...HONEY...LION!

A STORY FROM AFRICA

G. P. PUTNAM'S SONS ◆ NEW YORK

Copyright © 2005 by Jan Brett
All rights reserved. This book, or parts thereof,
may not be reproduced in any form without
permission in writing from the publisher,
G. P. Putnam's Sons, a division of Penguin Young
Readers Group, 345 Hudson Street, New York, NY
10014. G. P. Putnam's Sons, Reg. U.S. Pat. & Tm. Off.
The scanning, uploading and distribution of this book via
the Internet or via any other means without the permission of
the publisher is illegal and punishable by law. Please purchase
only authorized electronic editions, and do not participate in or
encourage electronic piracy of copyrighted materials. Your support
of the author's rights is appreciated. Published simultaneously
in Canada. Manufactured in China by South China Printing Co. Ltd.
Design by Gunta Alexander. Text set in Adriatic.
The art was done in watercolors and gouache.
Airbrush backgrounds by Joseph Hearne.
Library of Congress Cataloging-in-Publication Data
Brett. Jan. 1949— Honey...honey...lion!: a story of Africa /
Jan Brett. p. cm. Summary: After working together to obtain
honey. the African honey badger always shares it with his
partner. the honeyguide bird. until one day when the honey
badger becomes greedy and his feathered friend decides
to teach him a lesson. [1. Honey badger—Fiction.
2. Honeyguides—Fiction. 3. Symbiosis—Fiction.
4. Africa—Fiction.] I. Title. PZ7.B75225Hon
2005 [E]—dc22 2005000449
ISBN 0-399-24463-8
1 3 5 7 9 10 8 6 4 2
First Impression

IN AFRICA the honeyguide and the honey badger are partners when it comes to honey. The little bird follows a bee to its hive, and then she leads the honey badger there to break it open with its big strong claws. Together they share the sweetness. And that is the way it has always been.

Maybe this day Badger was hungrier than usual. Maybe he forgot about Honeyguide, who showed him the way. Or could he have been thinking: My strong claws do all the hard work. Whatever the reason, that day Badger would not share.

Honeyguide scolded Badger as he waddled back to the
Jackalberry tree, his tummy almost touching the ground.
She fussed and fumed as he tried to fit into his burrow.

Finally she cried out for all the animals
to hear, "No fair, no fair!"

Soon all the guinea hens were broadcasting
the news, "Honeyguide is in a major rage!"

But Badger didn't hear. He was sound asleep, smiling, snoring and hiccuping from his big meal.

"Grrrrrr-umph!" Badger roared out the loudest hiccup of all, and its deep, low rumble gave Honeyguide an idea.

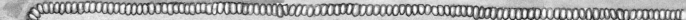

The next morning Badger woke up hungry, his tummy flat as a pancake. That's when Honeyguide flew by, heading for the great gray baobab.

"Honey, honey, honey!" she cried, grinning.

The little bird zigzagged over its large roots.

PITTER, PATTER!

Badger ran after her.

PITTER, PATTER!

Honeyguide flew low across the water hole.

SPLISH, SPLASH!

Badger paddled after her.

SPLISH, SPLASH!

Honeyguide glided to the top of a termite mound and bounced on one foot.   SPRONG!

Badger scrambled to the top
and bounced off.

SPRONG!

Honeyguide landed on a hollow log. It echoed as she stomped along. **BOOM, BOOM!**

Badger hurried to catch up. **BOOM, BOOM!**

Next Honeyguide flitted through a stand of papyrus. Tall, dry reeds waved back and forth. **CLICKETY-CLICK!** Badger traipsed along, muttering, "Where is that honey?" The papyrus rattled as he went by. **CLICKETY-CLICK!**

Honeyguide led him through a field of golden
bristle grass. **SWISH,
SWISH!**

Badger huffed and puffed, but the thought of
the delicious meal waiting for him kept him going.

SWISH,
SWISH!

By now Badger was tired and wet, itchy and sore. But he didn't slow down, because Honeyguide was just ahead of him. She flashed her wings, fanned her tail and dove under an acacia tree.

Badger charged in after her, singing triumphantly,

HONEY...HONEY...

LION, **LION**, *LION!*

Badger turned on his tail and ran.

SWISH, SWISH through the grass . . .

...**CLICKETY-CLICK** into the papyrus... **BOOM, BOOM** over the hollow log...

. . . **SPRONG** over the termite mound . . . **SPLISH, SPLASH** across the water hole . . .

. . . PITTER, PATTER over the baobab roots . . .

Badger dashed into his burrow. Honeyguide cheered.

In a flash Badger was as far from the entrance as he could be.

Right behind him was Lion's huge paw, batting the air.
But he could not reach him.

And that's the closest any animal could be to an angry
lion and live to tell the tale.

That evening Mongoose squeaked to Elephant, who trumpeted
to Hippo, who bellowed to Warthog, who squealed to Bishop Bird,
who piped to Hyena, who whooped to Zebra, who snorted to Giraffe,
who was overheard by Guinea Hen, who bugled it far and wide.
It was the bush telegraph, and it said, "If Honeyguide leads you
to a beehive, be sure and reward her, or next time,
she will lead you to a lion!"